HELEN MUIR

Wonderwitch and the Spooks

Illustrated by Linda Birch

MACDONALD YOUNG BOOKS

FOR ANNPAN AND HER GRANDSONS,
FREDDIE AND MICHAEL

The Ghost Train

Sometimes Wonderwitch grew tired of mixing spells, and talking to herself, and wanted some new adventures. One summer day, she went to a funfair with her old friend Witch Wotnot.

They had a turn on the Big Dipper and two goes on the Dodgems. But they went twelve times in the Ghost Train because witches adore rides in the dark.

"I like frights. Let's go again!"
Wonderwitch kept saying.

"Get in!" she called to the other
passengers, taking the front seat herself.

"Watch me make those old spooks
jump out of their skins!"

"Spooks don't have skins," Witch
Wotnot said.

Wonderwitch smiled slyly. "Wait till
I catch one, then we'll see!"

A boy in the Ghost Train queue pointed at her. "That lady lives in Wasp Court. She's always doing funny things."

"Shush, Marlon," said his mother.

The witches cackled as the Ghost Train rumbled off into a dark tunnel.

"*Eeeeeee…!*" Witches' screams are high and shrill. Something clammy touched their faces while a headless body floated past lit up by an eerie red light. Wonderwitch threw an iced bun at it. *Whapp!*

To her horror the train stopped beside
a dusty window from which a vampire
bat was peeping out at them. *"Ooooooo!"*
A shower of cobwebs sent the witches
rolling into each other as they lurched
off again. *"Owww…eeeeeeee!"*

Once the train picked up speed, spooks waited at every turn. A hollow voice laughed from nowhere, "HOO HOO HA!"

By the twelfth ride, Wonderwitch knew what was coming. She was ready for the grinning skeleton when it popped up out of a coffin. She whacked it with her handbag and knocked its head off!

The witches laughed so much they couldn't get out of their seats.

The funfair man was furious.

"You two ladies are to stay away from my Ghost Train. D'you hear me? You're banned!"

"Cheek!" Wonderwitch sniffed, as they went outside and got on the bus. "*Some* people!"

Wotnot agreed. "We bought twenty-four train tickets."

"Well, it's all right getting frights but, being a wonderwitch, what I like is giving 'em." And Wonderwitch whipped the vampire's mask from the ghost train out of her bag and put it on.

People stared in horror as the witches cackled together. Marlon was sitting behind them with his mother.

"I'd really, really like to look like that," he said.

"How shocking!" said his mother.

The Haunted House

Her rides in the Ghost Train gave Wonderwitch the idea of making all kinds of funny masks at home. She couldn't stop talking about ghosts.

"You know, there's a fortune to be made from giving people shocks," she told her black cat. "I could turn this place into a haunted house. After supper I'll look up some spells."

While the cat snoozed, Wonderwitch opened a book of frights called *Home Horrors*. "Heh, heh, heh!" she cackled. "I'll conjure up a real ghost to bring the crowds in."

She mixed a spell in her black cauldron and chanted some magic words.

"Come monster spook with eye of doom,
And clanking chains to pace the room,
Slide through my wall with ghostly power,
Show yourself at the witching hour!"

At midnight, with a gust of icy wind, a grey mist filled the kitchen. Objects flew about and after that there was a loud clanking on the stairs all night.

It put Wonderwitch in a rage because she couldn't sleep. Wherever she went, the ghost was hanging about clanking, ringing the doorbell or using her mobile phone. Sometimes she caught sight of a bloodshot eye looking at her in the shower.

"Go away!" she shouted.

"You called me!" The ghost tossed a bag of flour at her, "I've come for ever."

The curtains blew up in the air, the windows rattled and the clanking grew louder then ever. Wonderwitch rushed off to mix a spell strong enough to get rid of the troublesome spook.

"Get going now, ghostly pest,
My cat and I need a rest!"

At last, even the walls shook. Lights sizzled. The grey mist grew black and rained all over her. Then it was gone.

"Good riddance!" the witch said faintly, sinking into a puddle. "Who needs ghosts? Being a wonderwitch, I can pretend to be one myself because I know how to scare people. I'll practise on old Wotnot!"

Wonderwitch asked Witch Wotnot to come for supper and then she went shopping to buy a white sheet.

"I'll give her fish fingers and dandelion pudding. After that she'll pop upstairs to powder her nose and get the shock of her life!"

The meal went well. But after four helpings, Wotnot sighed, "Dear me! I can't move."

"Your nose is shiny. Up you get!" Wonderwitch picked up Wotnot's bulky old bag and gave her a push upstairs.

Then she wrapped herself in the sheet, put out the light and waited in the dark.

But Wotnot had had the same idea. In the bathroom she put on a black cloak and wig, and a nose and spectacles from the joke shop, with two fangs like a vampire.

When she was ready, she flung the door open. "WHOOOOOOO…" she cried. "Yum, yum! I smell blood!"

"*Eeeeeee…!*"

In her terror, Wonderwitch tripped on the sheet. She bumped into Wotnot who hit her on the head. Clawing and cursing, the witches rolled from the top stair to the bottom.

"*You?*" said Wonderwitch.

"*You?*" said Wotnot.

They couldn't stop laughing. Despite bruises and black eyes, they sat down together for another helping of dandelion pudding.

Witches' Night

Wonderwitch was lying on the bed, with the black cat on her tummy, eating jelly babies.

"It will be Hallowe'en soon," she said, "Witches' Night! I'll invite my friends to a fancy dress party. At midnight a ghost will appear. *Me!*"

The black cat sighed.

"We'll play duck apple and blind man's buff. I think I'll ask some children too. They love the old games and they'll tell everyone about my ghost."

Wonderwitch invited thirty witches. These included Witch Wotnot, of course, Witch Windbag (always last to leave), Witch Warthead (a cranky crone), Witch Wildblood and Witch Wonky. And she put up a poster in the park.

GRAND
HALLOWE'EN
FANCY DRESS
PARTY
AT WASP COURT ~ 31. OCT.
7.30

Marlon stopped to read it. "That's the lady in the Ghost Train. Can I go?" he asked his mother.

"No!" she said.

Wonderwitch made turnip lanterns for the party and hid itching powder and whoopee cushions about the house.

For supper there were sandwiches and samosas, jellies and ice-cream. She was just putting red apples into buckets of water for the first game when the witches began to arrive on their broomsticks.

Wonderwitch hurried out to greet them, rattling a money-box. "Welcome to Wasp Court!"

"Here we are!" cried Wotnot, looking like a vampire with her black cloak and fangs. Witch Windbag was wearing a cat suit. All the witches were in fancy dress and so were many of the children already coming up the drive.

"Strike me pink!" gasped Wonderwitch. There were such a lot of them.

The children told her their names as they filed into the house. Marlon, Freddie, Michael, Matthew, Daniel, Liam, Lucy, Lara, Samantha, Sarah, Dylan, Marit, Lani, Clare, Francesca, Alexander, Simeon, Megan…

"Trick or treat?" piped Megan, a small girl dressed as a witch.

24

"Trick," replied Wonderwitch, pushing her into a chair with itching powder on it.

"Where are the ghosts?" Marlon demanded.

The witch smiled. "Wait and see!"

The games started, but before long bangs and crashes were coming from upstairs as the children jumped out at each other in the dark.

The noise gave Wonderwitch a headache. "Supper time!" she called, hoping that food might shut them up.

The children helped themselves from a
long table in the kitchen while the witches
kept watch in case they finished off all the
toffee ice-cream.

"That Marlon's had five samosas,"
Warthead muttered crossly to Windbag.

"Mrs Wotnot," Megan asked, "why are
there so many brooms at Wasp Court?"

"Don't touch them!"

"Why can't I?" Megan stared at the
visitors' broomsticks piled in the hall.

"Never touch a broomstick on
Hallowe'en!"

"Why?" Megan tapped her witch's hat.
"I'm a witch. I need a broomstick."

"Steal a broomstick tonight and you'll
be carried off to the Olde Worlde, where
the witches live."

"Oh… *please!*" Megan begged.

"Silly girl," warned Wotnot grimly. "Once you see them, you'll be turned to stone. Haven't you noticed that little statue in the park? That was a child from the past who saw what he wasn't meant to see."

But Megan wasn't listening. She grabbed one of the broomsticks and dragged it to the door.

"*No!*" cried Witch Wotnot.

With a loud *whooooooosh*, she was gone. Some of the children screamed.

"Hey… brilliant!" Marlon said. He grabbed a broomstick too. "I'll get her."

"I'm not having a statue of that boy in my garden!" Wonderwitch mounted her broomstick and rose into the night sky with Wotnot and Windbag behind her.

"There they are!" As they spotted the children flying over gardens, Wotnot's black cloak blew right over her head and she crashed into Wonderwitch.

Wonderwitch bumped into Windbag. "Eeeeee… get off!" she screeched as she and Wonderwitch fell to earth like stones.

Wotnot couldn't stop laughing. She laughed so much that she fell off her broomstick too. All three lay groaning in a flower bed.

"Help!" wailed Megan as she was carried away over the trees.

Marlon zoomed after her.

"Let go!" he shouted. "Just drop!"

"I can't drop!" Megan clung to the broomstick. "I'll be hurt!"

Bruised and shaken, Wonderwitch narrowed her two black eyes to watch them disappearing into the clouds.

And after them, across the dark, moonlit sky, sailed all the other children on more stolen broomsticks. Wonderwitch nearly fainted!

She had to stop them meeting the merciless witches in the Olde Worlde or else her garden would be full of statues. But how?

Battered as she was, Wotnot had a brilliant idea. "It's too late to call them back. But it might work if we changed them into something else… something that can fly… quick, think!"

Wonderwitch started muttering.

"To Wasp Court you came and stole,
Now being a…
er… wasp will be
your role!"

Then the witches stood up and whistled into the wind for the broomsticks.

Seconds later, a cloud of wasps was buzzing round their heads.

Zzzzz... zzzzz... zzzzz...

"What a horrible party!" snapped Witch Windbag. Then she began chanting.

"Stop buzzing, wasps! It's time for bed,
Fall in a pile as if you're dead!"

"They're *my* wasps," Wonderwitch said crossly, "I'll look after them."

As the witches hobbled back to the house, quarrelling with each other, they spotted some people marching up the drive.

"Parents!" said Wonderwitch in a faint voice, and disappeared again.

She stammered out some words over the wasps.

"Wake up children! And it will seem,
What happened here was all a dream!"

One by one the children got up, shivered in the night air, then ran off home. Only Marlon, at the bottom of the pile, didn't feel the full magic force. He stopped at the gate and looked back as if he was trying to remember something ...

The Ghost of Wasp Court

After the Hallowe'en party at Wasp Court, the witches stayed in bed for weeks. Witch Wotnot's arm was in a sling and Witch Windbag was on crutches. Wonderwitch was bandaged all over. She did the cooking while the black cat shared his time between the patients.

"Never give a party with children or wasps," Wonderwitch said. "I'm still half-dead with shock. Luckily, being a wonderwitch, nursing comes naturally to me." She wore a uniform to empty bed pans and take temperatures and she pinned a notice on the garden gate.

Nursing – Quiet Please!

Just then Marlon kicked his football over her hedge. "Is your house a nursing home now?" he asked.

Wonderwitch shuddered. "Don't make a noise with that ball. My friends are trying to rest."

Marlon picked up his football. "D'you want me to help you?"

"No. Go away."

Afterwards she felt
sorry she'd said that.
There was a lot to do
in a house of moaning
witches, all lying in
bed watching television
and eating. They
wouldn't go
home because
they were
having such a
wonderful time.

When Marlon
came swooping
along on roller
blades, a few
days later, she
suddenly had
an idea of
how to get
rid of
them.

"Would you like to earn some money?" she asked and she told him her plan.

Marlon waited for an evening when his parents were out, then escaped while his older sister was on the phone.

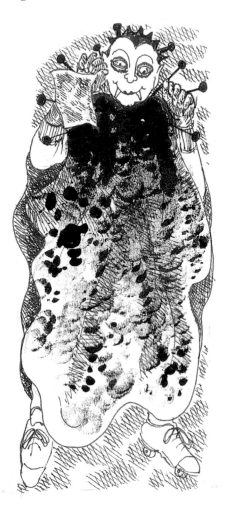

He skated round to Wasp Court where Wonderwitch was waiting with a five pound note, a most peculiar spook's outfit and one of her home-made masks. When he'd dressed up, he looked like a vampire from outer space.

"A Marlonspook!" she cooed. "Smashing!
Now glide around their beds waving your
arms but don't speak. They'll be terrified."

They weren't terrified because
they didn't wake up. Even when Marlon
tried stamping about in football boots,
they went on snoring. Wotnot did open
one eye. "Heh, heh!" she said and went
back to sleep again.

Marlon still hung about Wasp Court. "I bet you could make a lot of money out of a haunted house," he said.

Wonderwitch knew he was up to no good and wondered if anybody would notice if she turned him into a wasp again.

That night she heard noises in her garden and looked out of the window. People were running up the drive. By the light of the moon she could see a poster stuck to the gate. "SEE DARING GHOST – ONLY £1," it said.

She ran outside to find Marlon swooping through the air on *her* broomstick! "Strike me pink!" she said, wishing she *had* turned him into a wasp.

By that time Wonderwitch had had
enough of spooks. A haunted house was a
very bad idea if it meant all this noise in her
garden. She didn't want her house full of
witches either. And, as for that cheeky
child… well, she might miss him a little bit.

44

She stood still while she mumbled
a spell to send him home to bed... with...
er... a wasps' nest in it? No. Poor wasps!

The crowds waited for a while after
Marlon vanished. Then slowly they
drifted away, still talking about the
ghost of Wasp Court.

Next day, Wonderwitch and her black cat were far away. There was a For Sale sign on the house. Nobody bought it, of course, because it was haunted...

Look out for more spooky titles in the Red Storybooks series:

Wonderwitch by Helen Muir

Wonderwitch has all a witch could want. She has a tall hat, a black cat and a broomstick But when the black cat sits on a wasps' nest, she thinks it would be a good joke to have a sting as well...

Wonderwitch and the Rooftop Cats by Helen Muir

Every night, as Wonderwitch and the black cat ride on her broomstick, they can see the roofcats out on the tiles. And that's when Wonderwitch has her first brilliant idea.

Wonderwitch goes to the Dogs by Helen Muir

When Wonderwitch organises a dog race, there are four beagles, ten terriers, six dobermans, ninety-one mongrels and a sheepdog. None of the other owners realises that Wonderwitch has fallen in love with a stray greyhound...

The Twitches by Roy Apps

Gert and Lil are fed up. Although they've been witching for 113 years, they've never made up a successful magic spell. Something drastic needs to be done...

The Twitches' Chrissy-Mess by Roy Apps

It's Christmas Eve, and Gert and Lil are putting up their Chrissy-Mess decorations. There are spiders' webs, snail's slime, and a plate of mice pies and freshly-squeezed beetle juice for Father Christmas. It's bound to be a cackling good Chrissy-Mess for all.

You can buy all these books from your local bookseller, or they can be ordered direct from the publisher. For more information about Storybooks, write to: *The Sales Department, Macdonald Young Books, 61 Western Road, Hove, East Sussex BN3 1JD*